The

Ballad of a

Slow Poisoner

(A Tale of Great Spiders and Diamond Powder)

Andrew Goldfarb

Eraserhead Press
Portland, OR

ERASERHEAD PRESS
205 NE BRYANT
PORTLAND, OR 97211

WWW.ERASERHEADPRESS.COM

ISBN: 1-933929-60-X

Printed in the USA.

For Rani

Chapter One
Tea for One and a Half

Millford Mutterwurst sat down on a Tuesday to take his afternoon tea, and made the unpleasant discovery that his elbows were becoming flatter. "Sweet gobbling God," Millford exclaimed, examining the middles of his arms. "I could swear these were twice as pointy yesterday."

Millford was disconcerted, but wasn't going to let this ruin his tea-time. He daintily plucked twelve sugar cubes out of the bowl on his tea table and dropped them, one by one, into his cup. Joining him in this ritual was the fair Edweena Toadsweater, his paramour.

"Dear Edweena, would you say that my elbows have become flatter?" Millford inquired across the lavender tabletop.

"No, Millford, I don't think so." Her large, bulbous eyes gazed roundly outwards at Millford from either side of her nostril case. "Men like you are often afflicted by all manner of fancy, when more attention should be spent on manners and gardening. Take leave of this nonsense, and have another cup of tea," she implored, and poured, pushing another dollop of greenish and frothing liquid towards Millford.

Chapter Two

About Millford Mutterwurst

Millford Phelonius Mutterwurst made his living, in the United States at the top of the twenty-first century, by selling rocks from door to door.

Just this morning he had made a nice sale of a medium-sized chunk of boulder to a housewife on Crestfall Street. "I'm not interested in buying rocks," she had said. "Got no need for them."

Millford had quickly sized up the situation. His mole-like features, quite handsome on a mole but somewhat lacking on a man, became creased with concern. "Good Madam," he whined, "what you have failed to consider is the need that these rocks may have for you. Are we not all children of the vast Lump-Lump in the sky? Are we to remain isolated in the void, denied nutrients, as expendable as the draperies on which we were delivered? You may find yourself with no desire for companionship, but the same can not be said for the least mobile of our brethren."

In his particular field of employment, Millford was very much at the top of his game.

Chapter Three

About Edweena Toadsweater

Edweena Toadsweater, heir to the Toadsweater mouthwash fortune, hailed from the low country, where the swallows fly endlessly in short stunted circles.

Edweena first laid eyes on Millford at the thirty-first annual convention of the Nomadic Carpethuggers' Consortium (or NCC, for short), where he was displaying a fine roll of mustard-colored shag (this was prior to a mid-life crisis that resulted in his finding more gainful employment). Edweena was moved like a mountain. Pulling her auburn locks into a waffle shape, she had slithered to Millford's side and made a declaration of her intentions.

Chapter Four

"Until the End" (Edweena's Song of Love)

Snuff out the light, that I might see you better
It is your eyes I see when I close mine

This is the song I'll sing to you
Until the end (should it come)
Our last thoughts will be of love

We see stars fall, after all, don't be sad
Strange as it seems, you're the best dream I ever had

Chapter Five

The Demons That Hid Beneath Her Parasol

Having concluded their afternoon tea, Millford and Edweena went their separate ways. "Goodbye, dear Edweena," Millford sputtered, balancing curiously on one foot.

"Then I'll see you tomorrow, Millford," she replied.

"Yes, I suppose you will."

"Until then, then."

Edweena, having nowhere in particular to be, left Millford's ramshackle home and headed for the black beach at the edge of town, where she erected an umbrella to protect her from the gnawing attentions of the sun.

Edweena squinted upwards, and was surprised to see that dark clouds had formed above her; dark clouds, which now coalesced into the ominous shape of an elephant seal waddling towards her at an alarming pace. Sensibly, she dug a hole in the black sand and stuck her head in for a long while.

Chapter Six
Let's Not Go Splitting Chairs

The perceived flattening of his elbows had left Millford feeling agitated and confused. He puttered about with a mincing gait, attempting to slice the edges off of his furniture with a Prussian army knife.

"With my elbows gone, I'll have no need of these!" he babbled, hacking the arms off of his armchair.

Then, his energy expended, Millford gazed mournfully in the mirror. "I'm sure they were pointier yesterday," he reflected, caressing the thin narrows that connected his hands to his shoulder-stumps. To his benefit, he failed to notice that in addition to these troubles with his upper limbs, his ribs were concaving. His belly was as inverted as a bowl.

Chapter Seven

Slub Glub

Thirteen miles from the Mutterwurst residence, beyond the prickly thistles that routinely separate this side from that, dwelt the outcast hulk of the unusual Slub Glub. Slub Glub's rung on the evolutionary ladder was somewhere below both man and beast.

He had been born in a frying pan, raised by goat-herders, and employed as a door-knocker. "Turnstiles for the mustard gas," he used to say, as words never came easily to his rotund and sleepy countenance.

Tuesdays were Slub Glub's day for outings, and on this particular Tuesday he found himself crossing the prickly thistle and going into town.

Chapter Eight
The Unwanted Yodeler

As afternoon turned to evening and a veil of existential nothingness drifted closer to our little planet, Millford settled in front of his television set to watch a nature documentary about turd mice. It was while engrossed in learning about their complicated and demanding mating habits that he heard a faint yodeling coming from his kitchen.

"A little consideration, please," he hollered.

There was silence, and then a small and embarrassed "Sorry," which was a strong indicator that there was an intruder present, as Millford lived alone.

Chapter Nine

A Social Visit Gone Terribly Wrong

Entering his kitchen, Millford found the unredoubtable Slub Glub, who had one tentacle in Millford's jar of tea-bags.

"Excuse me?" Millford said, displaying great tact and restraint.

"Oh. I was just visiting my friends," Slub Glub said, embarrassedly placing the jar back in the cupboard.

"But I don't think we've met." Millford was befuddled.

"And I'm very pleased to meet you. Slub Glub, I think, is my name." Slub Glub looked up to face Millford (Slub Glub was a scant four and a half feet tall, contrasted with Millford's sixty-eight inches). Slub Glub's ordinarily bluish complexion was tinged with a green tint of shame.

"And I'm Millford P. Mutterwurst, but the point is, I don't think we're friends."

"Oh. My friends… They live in your tea bags."

Faced with such unfathomable news, Millford immediately forgot what he was hearing and returned to the other room, where he resumed watching his program. Slub Glub, no master of etiquette, followed along.

Chapter Ten
Love Among the Turd Mice

"The male turd mouse attracts the female of its species by secreting a luminous ooze from its nostril cavities, which it then rubs on its feet in a decorative fashion. Once adorned, the male turd mouse makes sporadic gyrations while emitting long, plaintive moans. The female will look for the male with the thickest coating of secretions on its feet, as well as the widest gyrations and most plaintive moans. The female turd mouse than signals her approval by plucking tiny hairs from her ear canal and offering them to the male."

Chapter Eleven
A Necessary Parting

A half an hour later, Slub Glub leaped to his feet with an effeminate yelp. "The conductor is without a compass," he said.

Millford looked around the room. "I don't see any conductor."

"It's a very small train," said Slub Glub, who was inching towards the door.

"Well, I appreciate your coming by."

Slub Glub paused at the entranceway, which was painted an unappealing salmon color, and looked Millford in the eye.

"I have a song for you."

Chapter Twelve

"Slide, Slide, Slide" (Slub Glub's Happy Song)

Slide, slide, slide
We all went for a ride
One of us got sick
One of us got rich

She went to see St. Augustine
At the front of a ruined hotel
Vines entwined the marble posts
That held up the ceiling before it fell

Slide, slide, slide
We all went for a ride
One of us got lucky
One of us got tricked

He came across some railroad tracks
Found a corpse behind a shack
Took a drink and danced a jig
Then walked away without looking back

Slide, slide, slide
We all went for a ride

One of us got married
One of us got sad

She wore a jewel between her thighs
Had the clerks cut down to size
Carried a head made of glass
Polished mirrors behind her eyes
Slide, slide, slide

Chapter Thirteen

An Unlucky Turn of Events

"That wasn't really a happy song at all," thought Millford, as he watched Slub Glub slump away with an unseemly lope. "No, I didn't like the sound of that one bit."

Millford meandered about the kitchen, polishing incidental implements of orange china, seeking to distract himself from the aftertaste of his recent houseguest. He was just working the grime off of a supper dish when a loud crash sounded in the next room.

Entering the sitting room, Millford was somewhat taken aback. Six black birds of prey had crashed through his picture window and lay comatose on the rug.

Chapter Fourteen

Birdie Buffet

Then, a knock at the door. Millford, by now convinced that the fates were playing him for a sacrificial lemur, approached cautiously, protected by safety goggles. He cracked open the door, and there was Edweena, wearing a lime paper dress, and holding a steaming teakettle.

"I figured tomorrow was too long to wait for our tea, so I brought some myrrh and chamomile. Mmmm... What's that smell?"

"Well, it's like pigeon pie, only it's made from vultures. Would you like some?"

"Why what a sweet surprise!"

And they sat down to a supper of boiled beaks.

Chapter Fifteen

An Omen of Ill Portent

Edweena gulped down another fork-full of the pungent grayish meat. "I say, Millford, this is very fine. Did you get it at the usual place?"

"No, as a matter of fact, six of them came crashing through my picture window this very afternoon."

Edweena spit out the contents of her mouth, which included not only half-chewed bird of prey but the aromatic tea as well, spraying a fine foam across the table. Apparently, Millford's comment had caused her some agitation. She stumbled to her feet, and swooned against the wall, banging her pendulous nose against the telephone.

"Edweena, what's the matter? I assure you, they're clean,"

"It's not that, Millford… It's the meaning of it all! We're doomed! The gods do not want us together."

"Edweena… I'm confused."

"The dead birds, Millford. They are like our love."

"Our love?"

"Oh, Millford. Why can't it be? When I pine and pine… But the world stands against us."

Chapter Sixteen

"I Walk A Lonely Road"
(Edweena's Song of Despair)

There'll be no hands a-knockin' on my door
The name you called me by won't work any more
All that I carry is a heavy load
I walk a lonely road

There'll be no kisses planted on my lips
Shave down the creases from my fingertips
From a frog to a prince back to a toad
I walk a lonely road

Through the cities and the towns
From sun-up 'til down
I walk alone, walk alone

Well you used to know me once
But even I don't know me now
I walk a lonely road

Chapter Seventeen

Limuhist, and Entanglements

"My, Edweena, I'm not sure what to say…"

Millford took their plates to the kitchen sink. He fidgeted by the freezer, while continuing to speak to Edweena in the next room.

"I wasn't aware of the extremity of your affections. I'm flattered, and yet…" He returned to the dining room, carrying an icy, lemon-colored loaf. "Do you care for some limwhist?"

Edweena nodded through her tears. Millford sliced both of them a thin ribbon of the sugary dessert.

"I appreciate you, Edweena, but you know… You know that I'm married to the sea."

Chapter Eighteen

About the Sea

Millford was indeed married to the sea, and not in the vague fashion of a sailor, but literally. Millford's mother, a gelatinous woman of angular proportions, had engineered this bizarre betrothal when Millford was a boy of seven years.

Mrs. Catipula Mutterwurst's motivations in this matter stemmed from her unhappy marriage to Millford's father. Millford's dad, a stooped man with cleft hands, had left Catipula many moons ago for a brazen young woman who worked under his supervision at the oyster factory. Mrs. Mutterwurst, intent on sparing her son such future heartbreak, had found him the perfect partner: the sea. Silent, strong, and immutable, the sea would never cheat on her dear boy.

And so it came to pass that Mrs. Mutterwurst, Millford, and a corrupt minister (who had been bribed with the promise of numerous shares in a bolt-manufacturing firm) held a strange seaside ceremony that left Millford a married man. Although the laws of their nation would not actually recognize such a union, Millford (and Edweena) remained unfortunately unaware of that fact.

Although his husbandly duties were few (the sea being reasonably self-sufficient), Millford did keep a painting of her body of water framed on the sitting room wall.

Chapter Nineteen

Edweena's Cup of Sorrows

Reminded that Millford was spoken for, Edweena cast down her eyes. "Well, let's just have another cup of tea, then" she muttered.

And they did.

Chapter Twenty
As If Rubbed by a Giant Eraser

That evening, before going to bed, Milllford made an unsettling discovery. His hands were shrinking. It had become apparent during his bath, when he could not get his fingers around the soap.

Upset, he went to sleep.

Chapter Twenty-One

Nightmare Theater

As soon as he fell asleep, Millford was plunged into the hideous vortex of his private dream world.

He was walking down the street in broad daylight… Everything was seemingly normal. Edweena was coming towards him along the sidewalk, though she hadn't noticed him yet. Millford waved casually. She didn't acknowledge him. "Odd," Millford thought, and he opened his mouth to call her name, but all that emerged were tiny bubbles.

Alarmed, he reached out to grasp her by the arm. In doing so, however, he saw that his arm had become so very thin that it was barely visible, and so weak that he missed Edweena entirely, and in fact stumbled into a patch of briar bushes on the side of the road. Edweena walked on by, completely oblivious to him.

On the upside, while entangled in the foliage, he did encounter some interesting bugs.

Chapter Twenty-Two

The Morning Dawns Dyslexic

While the sun slunk back up again, a cruel knocking was occurring at Millford's door.

His dreams had left him lessened, and he stumbled blindly through the house like a mouse trapped in jelly. "Go away," he moaned plaintively to his caller.

"Anyhomebody?" was the garbled response from the other side.

"I'm not buying any today," Millford said.

"Letmepleasehello," was the reply. Millford opened the door exasperatedly, and there was Slub Glub again, wearing a peach colored bonnet on his blue, lumpy head, and holding a wicker basket of posies in his left tentacle (from which protruded small suction cups, like an octopus). Millford resignedly let him in, and they sat down in the sitting-room.

"Posy?" Slub Glub asked, offering a flower.

"I'm withering away!" Millford exclaimed, displaying his tiny hands.

"Fleh?" Slub Glub gurgled.

"Disintegrating!" Millford exclaimed, holding up his elbows, which were so flat that you could balance a kettle on them.

"Wreth," Slub Glub noted, pointing an extremity towards Millford's chest. Millford looked down, and seeing the increased concavity of his torso for the first time, fainted dead away.

Chapter Twenty-Three
Roused From His Swooning

Slub Glub was fanning Millford with posies when the poor wisp of a man came to…

"Dear sweet babbling Bethuseluh, what's becoming of me?" he moaned.

"Perhaps you're dehydrated," offered Slub Glub thoughtfully.

"No, I don't think so… I've had plenty of tea."

Slub Glub got up and wandered towards the kitchen. "Maybe it's the wrong kind," he suggested.

Millford, remaining on the sitting-room floor, gazed up at the celing. "The wrong kind?"

"Green tea," Slub Glub called from the kitchen, over the sound of boiling water. "Green tea for you, and me, and monkey makes three."

Chapter Twenty-Four

That Which Had Been Not

And so Millford and Slub Glub sat down once more at the dining-room table. Slub Glub had brought bags of green tea in his peach colored bonnet, and they let them simmer in their cups.

"Flavorful," slurped Slub Glub.

"Quite," remarked Millford.

And so they sat, and sipped, and muttered. Then they sat some more, and sipped some more, and muttered some more. The morning sun arced towards the top of the world, and hung there domineeringly… And Millford and Slub Glub, after cup after cup after cup, settled further and further into their chairs, adopting the glazed looks of the excessive tea-drinker.

Then Millford detected the presence of a monkey at the table.

Upon further investigation, Millford decided that there was indeed a monkey present, sitting in the formerly non-existent third chair at the tea table, and it was scratching itself below the arm-pits. Millford stared at it in gaping-jawed shock. Slub Glub, apparently not noticing their recently arrived guest, continued to sip his tea and gaze blankly into space.

"We have a monkey among us," informed Millford, hysteria creeping into his voice.

"Yes" mused Slub Glub.

Chapter Twenty-Five
Difficulty of Comprehension

Millford put his cup down and questioned the monkey in an irritated fashion as to what it thought it was doing there in Millford's sitting room and how in Bethuseluh's name it had gotten there in the first place.

The monkey picked a fly from its head and ate it.

Millford peered more closely at the primate, and was surprised to find that not only had this monkey made a sudden and mysterious appearance in his house, but this same monkey was of a distinctly greenish hue, right down to its fur and eyeballs. It was also evident that the monkey was a male, although this in itself wasn't so surprising.

"Seems to me," mused Millford, "that I've heard of this sort of thing before, in a story perhaps..."

Chapter Twenty-Six
"Green Tea" (Millford's Song of Primate Response)

Sitting, sipping my green tea
A habit that I shouldn't keep

And the monkey's swinging from the chandelier
I can see through him, but not too clear

Perhaps it runs in the family
Like musty books no one should read

And you can keep your haloes to yourself
There are too many spirits on the shelf

I see your eyes
I see your yellow eyes
Gleaming in the moonshine from the sea

Scream all night
Yell and shriek and wail
Trying to catch a monkey by its tail

Chapter Twenty-Seven

A Cumulative Reaction

"A nice song," Slub Glub said. "Pass the sugar?"

Pleased at the compliment, Millford reached for the sugar bowl, but discovered that the request hadn't been aimed at him, but rather at the monkey, who had the sugar bowl clutched in his paw and was banging it on the top of his furry head, seemingly trying it on as a hat.

It was then that Millford noticed something particularly odd about his new houseguest… The outline of Millford's dining-room wall was poking faintly through the monkey's body.

As foreshadowed by his song, the monkey was a good deal less than opaque, and the tea table could be seen through the monkey's chest, as if the monkey-chest in question had been constructed entirely of green frosted glass. Thinking that perhaps it was just in his mind, Millford made a small test… He got up from his seat and went around the table to where the monkey was. Standing behind the furry animal, he peered at the back of its head, and through the soft green skull he could clearly see Slub Glub's corpulent form.

"It's a phantom monkey," Millford remarked.

Slub Glub looked over, and opined (to the monkey), "He's right. You do seem to be lacking in substance."

Millford contemplated this latest development.

Deciding that it was pointless to resist the steady slide into chaos that his life had become, he tore off all of his clothes and began leaping around the room like a jackrabbit, hollering at the top of his lungs.

Chapter Twenty-Eight
Impeccably Bad Timing

Edweena strolled up the street to the Mutterwurst residence just as Millford was overturning his tea table. Hearing the ensuing loud crash, and receiving no response to her fervent knocking, she poked her head against the side window to see what the commotion was about. She was then witness to the most shocking scenario her sheltered eyes had ever beheld.

Millford, wearing not a stitch of clothing, was now dancing the jitterbug on the top of his kitchen counter. At the same time, he was rummaging through his cupboards, cackling. He pulled out a frying pan. "We'll have no eggs today!" he screamed, and flung it to the floor. Then he took a fistful of vitamin bottles, and pouring them over his head, yelled, "Healthy healthy healthy!" in an unsettling falsetto.

As bizarre as Millford's behavior was, Edweena was even more shocked by what she saw in the next room: a ghostly green monkey, swinging from the rafters and emitting strange joyful squeaks, obviously pleased at the chaos occurring around him. Beneath the monkey, resplendent in peachy bonnet and blue complexion, sat the squat figure of Slub Glub, who was quietly sipping tea with one outstretched tentacle while holding his wicker basket in the other.

Edweena spent a moment or two in stupefied horror, and

then, regaining her composure, she marched on into the house, intent upon restoring order.

Chapter Twenty-Nine
Cruel Words Are Exchanged

"Millford Phelonius Mutterwurst! What in God's good name do you think you're doing?"

At that very moment, what Millford was doing was swinging a toaster by its electrical cord as if it were a lasso, while concurrently rolling among the refuse of his overturned garbage can. He paused in his exertions, and addressed Edweena.

"My hands are shrinking, my chest is inverting, my elbows are thinning, and I am being haunted by colored monkeys. Thus, I do this," he said, taking a carton of eggs from the refrigerator and cracking them under his armpits while emitting chicken noises.

"Well, stop it!" Edweena demanded. "Don't you remember that we had a date for tea? And here I am in my brand new dress, and you're parading around like... Like an ovulating hippopotamus!"

"Don't mind if I do!" Millford said cryptically, and he danced a silent waltz into the sitting room, where the monkey had taken to pouncing on the television and whooping. Millford joined him.

Edweena followed behind Millford, nearly hysterical. "Millford, if you and your friends can't behave like civilized individuals, I'm going to take my tea elsewhere!"

Slub Glub, who was still sitting at the tea table, said politely, "Oh, I wish you wouldn't go, madam, we were just about to have seconds." An aspect of Slub Glub's contrary character was that when events surrounding him became absurd, he was able to behave and communicate reasonably rationally; it was only under normal conditions that he would splutter and blather like a convulsive soup tureen. Edweena paid him no mind, however, as she was engrossed in observance of Millford and the monkey, who were holding hands and paws and were twirling in a circle atop the crumpled circuitry of the decimated television.

Edweena slapped Millford full on the face and stormed out of the house, a tear in her eye. Slub Glub, clearly dismayed at this upset, burst spontaneously into a mournful, enigmatic dirge.

Chapter Thirty

"He Who Gets Slapped"
(Slub Glub's Song of Domestic Discord)

His finest moment is shining
This oval mirror, its gilded display
With flesh and a voice, he's held captive
Chance meeting in secret, he's dressed up in his best

The high hand unknowing
The sea beast lays at rest
His fortune foretelling
Unleashing the lash
He who gets slapped

Her sterling virtue stands affronted
Their pendulum clock has now swung to a stop
Hawks have claws, the savage end, suspicion
She carves a smile on her powdered face from out of the box

The high hand unknowing
The sea beast lays at rest
His fortune foretelling
Unleashing the lash
He who gets slapped

Chapter Thirty-One
Getting Some Clothes On

"Of course, I'm not really dressed up in my best," mused Millford, looking sadly at his dilapidated, unclothed body, coated as it was with raw egg and television parts.

"Dressed! Fork blisters! I am nude!" shrieked Slub Glub, dropping his tea cup, apparently realizing for the first time that aside from his peachy bonnet, his short round blueness was exposed in its entirety to the elements. "Pickpockets! I must fix this at once!" He fished about in his wicker basket for a moment, displacing the posies, and pulled out a yellow muumuu, which he donned hurriedly. Millford sought to attire himself as well, and headed into his bedroom.

Millford's bedroom was a plain affair, as most of his time spent inside it was while he was unconscious, and thus he'd never really gotten around to decorating. The walls were colored an eggshell white, complete with cracks. The bed was of a folding variety, and existed in a state between compression and extension, making sleep an uncomfortable process. Millford's objective of the moment lay in his dresser, from which he extracted some woolly gray trousers and an undershirt, as well as a coat of indiscriminate origin.

The monkey opted to stay as God intended him.

Chapter Thirty-Two
The Call of the Hoofenfooter

Millford emerged from his bedroom to find Slub Glub and the monkey attempting to sweep up the mess that had been made. Watching them dispose of his television set into the garbage can, with Slub Glub behind a broom and the monkey erratically handling a dustpan, Millford's suspicion of the monkey ebbed. "He may be translucent," thought Millford, "but he's okay."

Millford sat down on the floor of the sitting room (all his chairs were smashed) and pondered his situation, taking mental note of the problems currently facing him.

First of all, his body had become adversarial and diseased. Secondly, he was in strong disagreement with his significant other. Thirdly, despite his guests' efforts at cleaning up, his house was a disaster.

With these issues looming over his head, Millford turned his thoughts to ideas of escape.

He listened intently for the faint sound of distant bugles, and the warm breeze that blows from the West; the signatures of the Hoofenfooter, the patron saint of the middling and beleaguered. The Hoofenfooter roams wild and free, unentangled in the bothers of the-day-to-day world, prancing aimlessly through the hills with its horns to the wind, and Millford desired to do the same.

"Fellows, stop your sweeping," he said. "I think it's time

46

we left the house." He was ready to run with the Hoofenfooter.

Chapter Thirty-Three
On the Way

Slub Glub seconded their departure as a fine idea, and he went off to the kitchen to get some tea to bring with them. The monkey picked more flies off his head.

Millford paused for a moment to contemplate the question of job responsibilities. If he did not make his rounds on Tuesday, bringing rocks to the neighborhood, would his livelihood disappear by Wednesday? "Probably not," thought Millford, and he sauntered out the door.

Slub Glub and the monkey followed closely behind, and when Millford stopped (because he did not know where he was going), they stopped as well. After another moment's pause, Millford, remembering something, moved decidedly around to the back of the house, where a sundry garden bloomed and withered.

The tomato plants were not in season, and therefore all they displayed were surly pale stalks, swaying despairingly in the afternoon dew. To their left, a mild assortment of weeds and seeds sprouted leafy contingencies about the backyard. This was Millford's garden, where nature had taken its wayward course and produced little that one could eat. Mostly there were drooping, thorny flowers with corroded leaves and tiny, purple berries, dangerous to birds and bees alike. "These would make a lovely tea," mused Slub Glub, but he was wrong, and Millford warned him not to touch them.

"Now, I'll show you something very special," Millford said, leading them to a very large structure a few feet distant. It was a barn.

"I didn't know you had a barn," said Slub Glub.

"That's because we've just met," answered Millford, astutely.

Chapter Thirty-Four
Big Rubber Thing

The monkey started saying "Whoop! Whoop!" as monkeys will do, and ambled into the barn and started climbing around the rafters. Millford and Slub Glub inspected the large, strange item that was the sole inhabitant of this wooden building. On the dusty ground was a huge, deflated balloon, of the aerial transportational variety. Its flattened form was made of painted rubber, and although crumpled and flabby, humanoid features could be discerned on its face. It had large, jubilant eyes, rosy cheeks, and a puckered mouth, all painted in bright and pinkish hues. This bulbous form was connected with ropes to a big basket, suitable for carrying people aloft.

Slub Glub touched its deflated forehead, then fell to the ground, wailing. "It's dead," he moaned.

Chapter Thirty-Five

Pumping the Beast

Slub Glub did not yet understand (and, actually, never would understand) that the dormant dirigible before them was not the extinguished remains of some large, round, once-living creature. "He's lost his insides!" Slub Glub blubbered, writhing tearfully on the ground, pawing at one of the rubber head's flabby eyeballs. "He's gone flat!" Upon hearing that last exclamation, Millford rubbed his elbows nervously, and felt a renewed haste to get on with their exodus.

"Let's blow it up," Millford said, a command that Slub Glub misinterpreted piteously, provoking more sorrowful moans, and a feeble attempt at prayer. Once he discovered that Millford wasn't sticking dynamite up its nose, but rather was huffing into a tiny hole in the painted lips, he regained composure and took hopeful turns with Millford in this mouth-to-mouth resuscitation.

And so Millford would breath deep, and then blow into the big rubber head, and then Slub Glub would do the same, and bit-by-bit the balloon became bigger, higher, and rounder. In this fashion afternoon passed into evening, and the monkey swung excitedly from the rafters as the giant dirigible face expanded towards him from below.

Chapter Thirty-Six

Necromancing

By the time that Millford and Slub Glub were out of air (and the balloon was full of it), the airship had grown so huge that it was as big as the barn, and there was no way that the craft could fit through the building's doors. They had to take axes to the walls and physically dismantle the barn, chopping at the wooden structure until the roof came crashing down around them and the four sides fell outwards into the garden. The monkey found this very exciting. Luckily, no one was hurt, and the resilient balloon didn't pop. The three creatures stood amongst the rubble and admired the great blimp, whose smiling head was an ample rival for the moon, which was now full above them.

"He's alive! He's alive!" Slub Glub was chirping, doing a little dance around the airship. "We cured him! We are…. Doctors!"

Slub Glub paused, awed by this realization of his and Millford's fantastic healing powers. He touched the cheek of the big blimp's face, whose pink shade shined radiantly in the reflected moonlight. "I shall name you 'Lumino.'"

Chapter Thirty-Seven
Plotting the Piloting

Millford, meanwhile, produced from the floor of the balloon's basket a cylindrical tube. It was about three feet in length, with an eyepiece on one side and an adjustable ring at the other. Millford peered upwardly through this device, in an attempt to project their trajectory across the night sky that awaited them. Unfortunately, this action, an emulation of some vague knowledge of the use of telescopes by mariners engaged in sea voyages, would prove to be misleading, as the optical device that Millford had procured was in fact a kaleidoscope.

Focusing on the myriad number of elliptical glass shards and colored sands as they reflected in the toy's mirrors, Millford called out to his compatriots. "We'll go that way," he said, pointing towards Mrs. Groghaven's apple orchard on Crestfall street. And then he got in the basket.

Chapter Thirty-Eight
Escaping Gravity's Clutch

The monkey and Slub Glub also got in the basket, although it wasn't easy for Slub Glub to climb into a basket while wearing a muumuu. But eventually, there they were: three would-be adventurers in a blimp, rooted solidly on the ground and staring up at the stars.

Some time passed, and clearly nothing was happening. Millford fiddled some more with his kaleidoscopic navigational instrument. Slub Glub hummed to himself. Then the monkey got out of the basket, and emitting the chirps and whoops of monkeyspeak, he rolled onto the ground, put his ghostly green feet up against the side of the basket, and started kicking.

Lumino bounced back and forth with the monkey's exertions, to a greater and greater degree, until it was swaying back and forth with such gusto that Slub Glub had to hold on to his peachy bonnet for fear of losing it. After more frenetic monkeypushing, the blimp gained enough altitude in its undulations that it was caught on a gust of the night wind, and rose mysteriously away from the Earth. The monkey latched onto the bottom of the basket as it teetered upwards, and swung himself inside.

Lumino lurched past the branches of one of Mrs. Groghaven's apple trees, nearly snagging a branch. Slub Glub and Millford congratulated the monkey profusely, and they headed off into the unknown, while Millford sang a little number he had composed for the occasion.

Chapter Thirty-Nine
"A Fine Day For Ballooning" (Millford's Freedom Song)

I'm not the man you thought you knew
And I've been working on a thing or two
People 'round here will think they're seeing things
And I'll be finding where the Westerly wind leads

It's gonna be big, big as a barn
And get up high, away from this farm

You've got your machines that make you move so fast
And get you nowhere while the time goes past
It's a lost art to be large and slow
Following where the westerly winds blow

It's gonna be big, big as a barn
And get up high, away from this farm

With my ballast and my goat
A sheep and a pig or two
Company to see the clouds through

Your patchwork land's behind me now
Headed for the sun

Like a star, fade in to the ocean

See a spot up in the sky
Can't close your eyes
I've learned to fly

Chapter Forty

Heaven for a Snack

At the close of Millford's number, Slub Glub, an emotional sort, had a tear in his eye. "That's the nicest song I've ever heard," he said, doffing his peach bonnet in humble deference. The monkey, however, was looking around for the aforementioned goats, sheep, and pigs, and disappointedly found none.

Once they cleared Mrs. Groghaven's orchard, the balloon rose steadily. Mrs. Groghaven had been in her sewing room at the time, knitting red socks for her third foot, when out of the corner of her eye she saw the much larger corner of Lumino's eye brush against her favorite apple tree. Assuming that the round countenance of the balloon, phosphorescent in the moonlight, was the spirited embodiment of the apple trees of her orchard taking flight into the unknown, she flung her knitting aside and stretched herself out beneath her porch awning, screaming, "Great Seeded Ghost! I Beseech You!"

But to the world below, the balloon had already faded to a speck. Mrs. Groghaven caught a fleeting glimpse of what appeared to be a monkey, and then it disappeared.

That night, two faces floated in the sky… The moon, with its old man's grimace, and Lumino, whose rotund pink pallor drifted through the ether as if hung from an invisible thread and pulled by slothful, portly angels.

As they rose higher and higher, and the deep blue of the clouded plane gave way to the inky blackness of the space, they found themselves navigating among the stars. Back home, Millford had always figured that stars were tiny points of light, but now that he saw them up close, he discovered that they were really large constructions of Styrofoam and tinfoil. The monkey took a large bite out of one as it floated by, but was persuaded to spit it out by Slub Glub, who was afraid that the great Lord Lump-Lump might be offended and would slap them back down to Earth.

A few hours later found the three travelers quite weary, and they drifted off to sleep, peacefully dreaming only of more sleep, and maybe some ice cream.

Chapter Forty-One
Thorn, Thistle, and Thrush

The next day found Edweena back at the Mutterwurst residence, teapot in hand. She was not at the door, but instead had first gone around the back, to the garden. She was kneeling by the berry bush, the same berry bush that Millford had warned Slub Glub away from. Edweena was oblivious to the ruined barn just to her left.

Ignoring the spotted bird carcasses that lay at her feet, and glancing nervously from side to side, she plucked the foul purple berries off of the branch and dropped them in her tea-kettle.

Chapter Forty-Two
"Let Go Of The Earth" (Edweena's Morbid Melody)

All the little boys and girls
The worms deep in the dirt
Every creeping thing will one day
Let go of the earth

Row your boat into the sea
See lights along the shore
Friends are waving hands at you
You won't see them no more

It all becomes quite evident
Too soon after your birth
That one day, don't know when
You'll have to let go of the earth

Funny way of doing things
But that's the way they work
Every creeping thing will one day
Let go of the earth
And float away

Chapter Forty-Three

Her berries all picked, Edweena was getting up to ring the door-bell, when she suddenly noticed how quiet the house was. Then she saw that Millford's barn had been chopped to smithereens. "Something," she thought, "is up."

"You bet your behind something is up!" said Mrs. Groghaven, reading Edweena's mind. "Your dang adulterous boyfriend is up, that's what's up!" she said, climbing over the fence and into Millford's yard.

Edweena looked at her quizically. Mrs. Groghaven, a stumpy matron of middling years, wore a yellow frump's coat and a permanent scowl. She sidled up next to Edweena and continued her disgruntled discourse. "He and his crazy buddies took off last night in their godforsaken flying machine, and nearly ripped the tops off my apple trees!"

After a long and trying dark night of the soul, Mrs. Groghaven had found that she was not yet ready for religion, and had discounted her initial tree-spirit explanation for the large head of Lumino that she had seen the previous evening. A more cynical analysis of her observations pointed towards the suspicious she-nanigans of her erstwhile neighbor, Millford Mutterwurst.

"Flying machine!" Edweena exclaimed.

"Yup. Dumbest thing I ever saw. Looked like a giant

clown head with a Dixie cup strapped to it. And now who's going to bring me my rocks? My cat'll run away if I don't get my rocks. And that's not the least of it." She eyed Edweena shrewdly, relishing her role as the bearer of bad news. "I guess you don't know yer lyin' lover quite as well as you thought."

"What do you mean?"

Mrs. Groghaven leaned in close, and Edweena could smell the gasoline on her breath. "He was consorting with monkeys," she said.

"Do you know which way they went?"

Mrs. Groghaven stuck her sizable nose in the air, and with a snort, pointed one of her stubby fingers westward. "They went that way... Towards the sea."

Chapter Forty-Four

Balloonatics

Morning found our three travelers revived, refreshed, and significantly lost. Lumino had dipped back down below the stratosphere, and as Millford looked about, all he could see was a vast expanse of blue. "My wife!" he thought. He ducked down out of sight. After a few minutes, though, it occurred to him that they were probably too high up to be spotted by the sea, and he relaxed.

Without a dot of land in sight, it was now clear to the trio that this journey, wherever it may lead, was likely to take a while. Therefore, some pragmatic issues needed to be worked out.

After a short discussion (to which the monkey's contributions were minimal), it was agreed upon that for the duration of their airborne travels, no bodily functions would be permitted. There simply wasn't enough room. The second pressing matter was that of food. Slub Glub had had the presence of mind to bring along a jar of nutmeg and some toast (without butter, unfortunately), and the monkey managed to catch a flying fish, but beyond that, there was nil.

Nil, that is, save for a nearly unlimited supply of tea, which Slub Glub had thoughtfully liberated from Millford's kitchen. By distilling water from a passing cloud, and heating it with the eyepiece from Millford's would-be navigational kaleidoscope (which channeled the rays of the sun nicely), they were able to boil pot after pot of tea. And so they did.

Chapter Forty-Five
To the Deep

Edweena followed the trajectory to which Mrs. Groghaven's fingertip had pointed; that path eventually brought her to the beach.

She stared at the sea, looking her rival in the eye, and with a quiet determination, decided that no big drink of water was going to stand between her and her man.

After a short search, she located a boat rental outfit, and without much ado she set out to brave the big blue waters, alone, in a rowboat, with naught but her teakettle.

Chapter Forty-Six
A Cup of Sorrows

Millford was concerned about his eyebrows. Since he had been aloft in Lumino, Millford had thought little about the physical deterioration that caused him so much concern back home. However, while drinking his tea today, he saw one small dark hair, and then another, drop into the steaming beverage, and it wasn't long before he whined aloud the realization, "My eyebrows are thinning!"

Millford felt a renewed urgency to get wherever they were going. He had the common, vague hope that if he got far enough away from home, he would leave his troubles behind. But at this rate he'd fade into oblivion before they had a chance to arrive anywhere. Millford extracted his cylindrical tube from his pocket, and with his eye to the glass and his hand on the rotating ring, declared, "I calculate a northernmost hemispherical latitude crossing by the starboard wind factor of naught ought six. Let's set us down…there!"

Millford pointed to a spot on the horizon, a spot that, to everyone's excitement, got bigger and bigger as they approached, eventually becoming a very large spot with palm trees and little houses on it.

Chapter Forty-Seven
Ambassadors of the Strange

Millford reached up to Lumino's lips and opened the small aperture between them, letting out a slow current of air from the great rubber head. This deflated the blimp just enough to allow a gradual descent downwards. As this happened, though, Lumino also made a tremendous, seemingly endless, farting sound, a thousand times greater than any ordinary deflating balloon.

Down below, the inhabitants of the small island were indoors, taking a siesta. Their naps were interrupted rudely by this great flatulence from the skies, which began as a faint raspberry but grew to a roar as Lumino descended on their village. The villagers left their beds and came outside to see what the fuss was.

Lumino was nearing the ground; his wide eyes and beaming smile bore down rapidly on what appeared to be the small island village's central courtyard. Millford and Slub Glub waved excitedly from the basket, and the monkey jumped around, screeching and whooping.

The island's inhabitants immediately recognized Lumino and its crew for what they were…three weirdos in a big rubber balloon. Nonetheless, the villagers were a hospitable lot, and came forward to greet them.

"Buenos dias, amigos. Como estan?" said a gentleman in a floral shirt and tan slacks, sombrero and sandals. His smiling chin bespoke an easygoing nature, and he held out his hand for shaking.

Millford was about to speak, when Slub Glub held him back with a tentacle, whispering, "Let me do the talking. I speak their language."

Chapter Forty-Eight

"Todo Es Mal" (Slub Glub's Song of Bilingual Outreach)

El diablo es aqui!
Mi nombre es muerte!
Que dia de miserable!

Todo es mal!

El vampiro del amor!
Estoy el gringo loco!
Un disastro de electricidad!

Todo es mal!

Nosotros somos los monstruos!
Nosotros somos los monstruos!

El libro siniestro!
Fruta macabra!
O no mi cabeza!

Todo es mal!
Todo es muy mal!
Todo es muchos, muchisimos mal!

Chapter Forty-Nine
Communication Breakdown

Millford, whose grasp of Spanish was even shakier than Slub Glub's, didn't know what had just been said, but guessed from their hosts' reactions that it wasn't good. As Slub Glub stood proudly, the villager, who now looked disdainful and suspicious of them, withdrew his hand and slowly backed away. The other townspeople, with jaws a-gape, did the same, walking quietly backwards into their homes and closing their doors behind them. Soon they had returned to their siestas, and the three travelers stood alone in the courtyard.

With a mutual shrug, Millford and Slub Glub began re-inflating their airship. Meanwhile, the monkey was whooping about excitedly, pointing to the trees and tugging on Slub Glub's muumuu. There were coconuts in those trees, and all monkeys know that coconuts mean good eatin'.

Chapter Fifty

Edweena, in the Eye of the Maelstrom

The sea was not pleased to have her husband's lover trespassing across her waters, and responded accordingly. Starfishes were tossed at Edweena's nose. Choppy waves rocked the little rowboat to the point of Edweena's nearly losing her lunch. Edweena bore this humiliation and soldiered on, rowing steadily on the course that she had set, certain that Millford must be somewhere ahead of her, flying over the immense surface of his wife.

It was during one of the sea's tantrums, which manifested as a twisting typhoon, that Edweena picked up a hitchhiker. The angry water was breaking around her in walls of foam and displaced clams, and her boat was spinning like a top, gripped in the circular whirlwinds of jealousy. Hers, however, was not the only craft being bullied by the malevolent tides. A dilapidated lifeboat was twirling around as well, submerging and re-emerging and generally getting all topsied and turvied. By the time the sea's fury was spent, a very wet Edweena found her rowboat alongside this dinghy, which turned out to be occupied. Aboard it were a ventriloquist's dummy and a corpse, both of whom wore very soggy tuxedos.

Chapter Fifty-One

Gone Coco

"How many coconuts," Millford wondered aloud, "are too many?"

"Too many coconuts," Slub Glub echoed with an anguished moan. In the two hours since their departure from the island, with island fruit in tow, copious amounts of coconuts had been consumed. Slub Glub, already a portly character, had become positively lumpy as a result of this culinary over-exertion. It probably didn't help matters that he failed to chew the said coconuts, but rather slurped them down whole, as if they were oysters (Slub Glub had a flexible and accommodating mouth). He fanned his flushed blue face with his bonnet, while wearing a coconut shell on top of his head. A trail of coconut milk drifted down his left cheek.

The monkey had created a stack of cracked coconut shells from which he had enthusiastically drunk. Hours into their feast, the monkey was still gulping down the white and syrupy contents of the coconut fruit.

Millord had mistakenly theorized that by increasing his calorie intake, he might stave off the mysterious whittling that was reducing him to a shadow of his former self. Although he had eaten enough coconut meat to choke a wrestler, his extremities still dangled off his body with a stringy frailty.

Despondent and fatalistic, Millford rotated Lumino's big head and set it on a collision course with the sun.

Chapter Fifty-Two

Approaching the Big Orange

The monkey was the first to notice that things were getting hotter. Although his tummy had been sated, he continued to crack open coconuts, pouring the milk over his fuzzy head in an attempt at keeping cool.

"Say, fellows, did one of you turn up the thermostat?" Slub Glub asked. He was fanning himself exhaustedly with his peachy bonnet. Grossly, his muumuu was drenched with sweat. Millford was stoic, staring upwards with a manic gleam in his eye. Slub Glub followed his gaze, and when he saw what Millford saw, he let out an unseemly shriek.

They had once more ascended higher than the Earth's atmosphere. Millford had been tossing coconut shells overboard, lightening their load, in order to speed their upward progress. Now, the surface of The Sun was looming before them, a great fiery field of furnaces, a huge orange orb whose unpleasant hotness was matched by a disturbing aroma, similar to that of rotten eggs being fried.

As they drifted closer to this most familiar star, bizarre truths about that glowing fireball were revealed. First of all, the entire thing was not a blazing rock of burning stuff, as it appeared from the earth. As they came within spitting distance, they found a few stretches of solid ground that, although crusty and pockmarked, were not molten or a-flame. They managed to land in such a spot, which was a perilous process, as they had to dodge the high fires and yellow sparks that were all around.

Another strange realization was that although the sun was certainly damnably hot, sweltering even, it didn't melt them straight away. The monkey's fur was singed, certainly, and Millford had to remove his shirt. He did so reluctantly; his body had become so emaciated that the moles on his back could be seen through his chest. Overall, though, the atmosphere was not really that much less hospitable than Arizona in the summer.

Slub Glub was positively thrilled, and was the first to hop out of the balloon basket. He doffed his muumuu and spread it on the ground like a blanket. "This is the ideal time for me to work on my tan," he said, but he was wrong. Before his flabby blue skin had a chance to darken to purple, his muumuu caught fire. The sun's atmosphere itself may have been bearable, but the surface ground was red hot. Slub Glub leaped back into the basket, and there the trio remained, gazing out upon the strange landscape, trying to make sense of it all.

Chapter Fifty-Three

Keeping the Home Fires Burning

"Well, this is a strange sort of place," said Slub Glub. He had put out the flames on his muumuu, and though it was slightly singed, it was not much the worse for wear. The experience had rattled him, though, and he clutched his bonnet to his chest anxiously as he peered at the weird surroundings. The monkey, also, had decided that he didn't much like the heatedness of it all, and perched himself on Slub Glub's head, whimpering and squawking.

Lumino had landed on a patch of parched orange ground about a hundred feet around. The smoky, hazy air made it difficult to perceive what was beyond that space. It seemed that they were surrounded by fire, but it also seemed to Millford that there was something below the fires, but above the ground. "Could those be trees?" Millford wondered. "Could it be that the sun is one great forest fire?" He took out his kaleidoscope, attempting to glean more information. Then putting that aside, and squinting avidly, he saw that the trees were not trees at all, but shadowy humanoid forms, from whose tops the fires sprouted. He related this information to Slub Glub, whose opinion was that they should now be headed for either the North Pole of earth or, barring that,

to the Planet of the Ice Cream Sandwiches.

Unswayed, Millford cupped his hands around his mouth and shouted loudly, "Over here!"

It wasn't long before there was movement. Peering through the surrounding fires, the three travelers saw strange figures emerging from the haze. There was a group of humanish-looking creatures coming their way, orange of skin, lacking in clothes, and each holding a very large, flaming pyre in its hand.

Three were male, and two were female, and all wore identical solemn expressions on their faces. They hardly moved; only their feet did a slow shuffle in the direction of the balloon. Their eyes were glassy, and didn't seem to be focused on the three balloonists. The sun people are Zombies, Millford hastily surmised.

"Hello," he said, but none of them answered. More seemed to be emerging from the haze, all carrying big, burning sticks, and wearing the same inscrutable expression. With a sickly sensation, a grim realization dawned on Millford. This must be what generates the sun's heat. A legion of drones carrying torches.

"So," Millford said, addressing the lot of them. "This is what you do."

They did not reply. More distressingly, they did not stop. The sad, slow, orange folk moved closer to Lumino, wielding their flames perilously close to his pink, rubber face. The three travelers were encircled by dozens of these blazing, orange smokers, and more were emerging from the surrounding blazes every second. Recognizing the danger of their situation, Millford fell into a stupor. Slub Glub broke down in fear, cringing in a corner of the basket. Luckily, the monkey had the presence of mind to take the offensive, and began hurling the remaining coconut shells at them.

Not accustomed to being pelted by flying objects, this slowed the attack of the sun people. In addition, the resultant lightening of Lumino, once the coconut shells were all dispersed, made for an ascension from the ground, and Millford, Slub Glub, and the monkey made a narrow escape from the horrible clutches of the sun and its strange, sorrowful citizens.

Chapter Fifty-Four
Driftwood

Edweena leaned into the lifeboat to inspect its cargo. She felt for the pulse of the dead man and discerned that he was, indeed, dead. She then felt for the pulse of the wooden dummy, and found a faint, though irregular, beating. She hauled him into her rowboat, and let the lifeboat drift away with its morbid cargo.

Edweena took a closer look at her guest. He was about two and a half feet tall, made of pine, and very snappily attired, with spotted bow tie and miniature formal dress. His eyes were big, wooden, and rolling, and his jaw, beneath painted teeth, was hanging askew from a rusty hinge. Seeing that he was soaked with salt water and unmoving, she attempted mouth-to-mouth resuscitation, blowing her hot air into the dummy's mannequin maw. In moments, it sputtered to life, it's eyeballs spinning and limbs flailing, and it burst spontaneously into song...

Chapter Fifty-Five

"The Artful Ventriloquist"
(Grinnin' Gertie's Song of Show Biz Tragedy)

When your hinges come unscrewed
I will speak for you
When your tongue is tied up by a string
I will do the talking

The same reclusive figure in the balcony
Gazing at the puppet on his knee

Is she here for me?
Or just the wooden man I seem
If this wired jaw could speak clearly to her face
There would be no need to hesitate

The same reclusive figure in the balcony
Gazing at the puppet on his knee
Every performance I am sure
This hollow head is singing just for her

Hurry through the stage door before the lights come on
Declining every encore, ignoring the applause

Unopened invitation from the lady in the box seat
I'm afraid we should not meet

When your hinges come unscrewed
I will speak for you
When your tongue is tied up by a string
I will do the talking

Chapter Fifty-Six
Rude, Crude, and Carved

Edweena was surprised and confused by this melodious outburst. She stared at the dummy, who had returned to a catatonic state. He smiled vacantly; a creepy, fixed grin. Edweena shook him by his wooden shoulders, but the puppet remained unresponsive. Thinking to inspect him more closely, she pulled him onto her lap, at which point he came instantly to life.

"Well, what have we here! A pretty lady, all adrift at sea! And not a shark in sight!" the little wooden man chirped obnoxiously, ending his absurd flirtation with a whistle. Edweena slapped him hard on the hinges.

"Sorry," he said. "I've been trained to talk like that."

"By who," Edweena asked skeptically.

"By… Hey! Where's Red?"

"Red?"

"Yeah! The fellow I was with! Looks like me, only larger?"

"I don't know how to tell you this…" Edweena began.

An immediate understanding came over the wooden man, and he hung his oversized head sadly.

"I should have known it would end this way," he said.

"Perhaps it would do you good to talk about it," Edweena suggested kindly.

Chapter Fifty-Seven
Limelight Failure Follies

"I met Red, oh… It must have been eight years ago, at a nightclub in Minneapolis. I was working with an old comic named Uncle Wally, and we were plumbing the after-dinner circuit. Red was on the bill, doing his standup. He had a solo act back then. He and I got to talkin'… We stayed up all night, playing cards, discussing the business; we really hit it off. Next thing you know, he and I had paired up, and we were doing pretty good. Some theater gigs, even an occasional T.V. spot. Maybe you saw us on "Wake Up Laughing," last year?"

"No, I don't think so," Edweena said, trying to remember.

"Well, like I said, things weren't going too bad. Much better than with Uncle Wally, anyway. That old geezer lived on gin and eggs, if you know what I mean."

"No…"

"The trouble began about nine months ago, in Philly. We had a week's run at the Philosopher's Club, and it's a small joint, maybe fits twelve, fourteen tops. Good crowd, though.

"Anyway, we get to doing the Rutabaga routine. That's the one where I'm supposed to be a starving. That's a laugh! You ever try eating with solid pine stomach?"

Edweena shook her head.

"To which Red says, 'I got a nice rutabaga here.' And I say, of course, 'No, I haven't been there, but I hear it's nice!'"

The dummy paused, apparently expecting some sort of reaction. Getting none, he pressed on with his narrative. "The point is, during this show, I notice a woman up in the stands. Fur coat, pearls, the works. And a knockout. Not one of those show biz types, you know? She had class. Both me and Red, we can't keep our eyes off her. Almost blow the routine.

"So, that's all very nice, but we don't think any more about it, right? I mean, we're on the road thirteen months of the year, we haven't got time for courting, not with a gal like that. But the next show, she's there again. In the same seat, watching the same gags as the night before, and laughing at 'em all like she's never heard 'em before. Weird, right? But to a comedian, that's powerful stuff, y'know? And she does it again the next night, and the night after that, and for the rest of our run there, she's at every show! Still laughing, still clapping. And Red, he's falling for her, big time. Can't sleep, eats only marmalade. But he doesn't do anything about it; that's not his style. Not at all. Without me, that boy was a wreck. Couldn't ask for a check at a restaurant. I did everything for us.

"Well, the last day of our run, the stage manager brings us a letter. And it's from her. An invitation to meet her after the show, and I tell him, 'Let's do it!' Mind you, I've never much been one for the ladies, no reflection on yours truly. It's my size, you see…"

Edweena shifted uncomfortably. The puppet was on the heavy side, and her thighs were starting to ache.

"But Red, being Red, sends her a note back, saying, no, he can't meet her, he's gotta pack for this cruise ship we're doing, maybe some other time. Which was true, actually. We were booked for a month on the Carnival Queen, shuttling from Florida to Paraguay. That's the boat from which you found us adrift, darling. But that comes later.

"So, we hustle out of Philly, get on a plane, get on the boat, get out to sea, and who do you think is on board?"

Edweena thought for a minute. "The woman?" she asked.

"Bingo. And she's hanging back, acting like it's just a coincidence, and Red's so shy, he's buying it. But I talk him into making a date with her. I say, 'Red, she ain't gonna bite you.' Of course, I was a dummy."

Edweena nodded sympathetically.

"So we go to her room, right? And we get to talking. And the problem is, it's obvious that she wants no part of him. She didn't have a thing for him, after all!" The little man paused, touched with emotion. "She wanted me."

He was choked as he finished his tale. "So he's so humiliated, he can't face the rest of the cruise. He wakes me up in the middle of the night, drags me outside, and throws us both in a lifeboat. An hour later a storm comes along, and that was all she wrote. Maybe it was the sea that killed him, maybe it was heartbreak."

Chapter Fifty-Eight
Introductions, Explanations, Ruminations

"That's so sad," Edweena said, dabbing her eye with a hanky from her purse.

"Yep," the dummy replied, regaining his composure. "So, darling, what's your story? What brings you out to this neck of the woods?"

"Well, I…" Edweena began, but her voice trailed off, not sure how to explain the tortured path of her recent past.

"Why don't you start with your name," the puppet suggested.

"Oh! Edweena Toadsweater. And you are?"

"The one and only Grinnin' Gertie, at your service, Ma'am," he said, giving a little bow from her knee.

"Well, Gertie. I'm looking for my boyfriend."

"I see," Gertie said, taking a look around at the water that stretched out on all of sides of them for as far as the eye could see. Taking a closer look at his newfound companion, with her elongated nose, wafflish hair, new dress and teapot, afloat in the middle of the sea in a rowboat, he reflected that it was quite likely that her sparrows weren't nested, so to speak. "Your boyfriend… He's a fish?"

"No, no, he's ballooning."

"Oh."

Chapter Fifty-Nine
At War With The Gods, And Losing

A suicidal impulse led him to navigate towards the sun, but now that they had escaped the doom that awaited them there, Millford was feeling somewhat more optimistic.

His cheer was misplaced, however, as just an hour later, a watery grave was to open up its soggy sarcophagus to them.

"Ooooh… Penguin," said Slub Glub, misunderstanding the species of bird that was flying next to Lumino. A Speckled Hornswallow was flapping along, its great florid feathers molting in the wind. "Must be migrating," mused Millford. The monkey hopped over to see what all the fuss was about, and the site of the translucent green monkey, through whom one could faintly see the clouds, freaked out the Hornswallow rather severely. The bird's flight pattern became suddenly erratic. This, in combination with an unfortuitous gust of wind, caused a collision to occur; the Speckled Hornswallow's great beak was buried deep into Lumino's rubber cheek.

A sickly whistling sound began to emanate from the point of insertion. "Don't move!" Millford said, addressing the hapless bird.

"If only I had some chewing gum," said Slub Glub, poking around in his basket for some sort of adhesive. The bird looked at them with embarrassment and horror.

91

The whistling continued, however, and Lumino's bulbous head began to slowly shrivel. His rosy pink cheeks were starting to resemble the drawn features of a fashion model, and wrinkles of concern appeared upon his once-youthful brow. A severe drop in altitude occurred. The clouds drifted by them in a vertical stream, and the Earth's blue, wet surface came careening closer. Sensibly, Millford, Slub Glub, and the monkey began to wail like schoolboys stuck with tacks.

They landed in the sea with a bracing splash, submerged partially in the salty fluid. Once they bobbed to the surface, wet and irritable, they found themselves floating aimlessly. "Uh-oh," said Millford, and he was right. They were three lone aviators in a fallen balloon, whose flabby rubber head was now lolling on its shrunken side in the sea, dragged behind the basket, which was, temporarily anyway, decent enough to float.

Slub Glub, who was severely depressed by this latest predicament, noticed that the Speckled Hornswallow still had its head stuck inside the badly deflated blimp. "This is all your fault," Slub Glub said solemnly, to the very guilty-looking bird.

Chapter Sixty

Not the Best Situation

The waters of Millford's wife stretched out endlessly around them. Millford pondered making excuses to his betrothed, and perhaps asking for a favor or two, but first the trio had a brief discussion as to whether they could perhaps find a way out of this on their own. However, not finding any solutions forthcoming, the three travelers decided to take a nap.

In the hour that passed, no problem-solving ideas were visited upon them in their sleep, though Millford did have a pleasant dream involving a house made of caramel, and the monkey had an unmentionable one involving another monkey that he used to know. Slub Glub, however, suffered through a nightmare in which he was eaten by an alligator.

Unfortunately, this nightmare mirrored reality rather closely, as Slub Glub was indeed being eaten by an alligator.

Awakened suddenly to find his stubby blue legs knee-deep in the jaws of a great green lizard, who was right there in their balloon basket, Slub Glub's shocked brain burst into song, a confused song that mirrored his emotions of the moment.

Chapter Sixty-One
"Alligator!" (Slub Glub's Song of Shock)

Your shrunken head
In a powdered wig
Black matchstick mole
Bum out on the dole
Your stopwatch silver chain
In a basket of brains
lions are tamed
Roast spit on a flame

Alligator!
Demonstration model six
You're my fix
Oooh… Aquamarine

Gung ho Gunga Din
Where everyone wins
Those silver spires
Impaling the choir
Fish fish fishy fish
Here's for what I wish
Three figs in a dish

With Lilian Gish

Alligator!
Demonstration model eight
You're my bait
Oooh… Aquamarine

Chapter Sixty-Two
Crocodilicious

"You're not well," Millford said to Slub Glub. Slub Glub blubbered and pointed to the alligator, whose toothy grin was closing around what would have been Slub Glub's kneecap, if Slub Glub's knees had been capped.

Just as things were looking grim, the monkey again came to the rescue. The furry primate clamped its phantom jaws down on the alligator's scaly tail. Though less than solid to the eye, the monkey teeth proved real enough to make for a mean bite, especially in quest of scaly meat that tastes like chicken. The alligator, receiving a taste of its own medicine, opened its mouth to groan, which gave Slub Glub the opportunity to slither out from inside the gator's slimy gullet.

The monkey kept on chomping at the green alligator's bottom, and the gator kept groaning. Moments later it crawled back over the side of the basket and into the depths from which it came. Millford heaved a sigh of relief. Slub Glub fainted in the corner. The monkey tried to jump into the water to chase after his lost meal, but Millford held him back.

Chapter Sixty-Three

Tea for One

Back in the rowboat, Edweena was lazily pulling the oars, while Grinnin' Gertie sat on her lap. Hours had elapsed since their respective life stories had been discussed, and there was no sight of balloons, land, or anything in particular, other than rolling waves. The sea no longer seemed to be concerned with Edweena's presence, and rather than throw obstacles in her way, it just left her to drift aimlessly, doomed to a slow starvation and/or dehydration and/or death by boredom.

Thinking of starvation and dehydration, or maybe just the boredom, Grinnin' Gertie turned to Edweena. "You wouldn't happen to have a nice Limwhist sandwich on you?" he asked. She shook her head. He then noticed the teapot that Edweena had brought along. "Hey, is that tea you've got there?" Edweena nodded. "Mind if I have some?"

Edweena nodded again, although her head may have just been bobbing with the rowing motion her arms were making. In any event, the dummy reached for the kettle and poured a fair helping of its contents into its mouth.

"Don't you want any?" he asked. "You must be thirsty by now, being human and all."

Edweena shook her head. "Yes, but not for tea. And I

97

thought you were made of solid wood," she commented.

"Oh, yeah, I know. It makes my hinges rust, too," he said, as the tea that hadn't soaked into his body dribbled down his shirt front. "But I've got a weakness for the stuff, even though I know it ain't good for me."

How right he was.

Chapter Sixty-Four
The Seven League Itch

Millford peered over the side of Lumino's basket, and stared at the vast body of water before him. It was time to explain things to his wife.

"Well, darling, you see… We married at such a young age. And what do we really have in common? With you so blue, and me so pale…"

Slub Glub, overhearing this comment, was a bit taken aback, being blue himself. The sea, however, was silent and impassive. Millford continued, fumbling for his words.

"The truth is, I was never really in love with you, and I doubt that you were with me. I mean, how many times had we met, prior to our engagement? There was the time I came down to build a sand castle as a child, and that brief experiment with surfing, in my teens, but even that ended with a broken leg…"

The sea appeared reflective, which wasn't unusual, it being a sunny day, but she seemed thoughtful, as well. Sensing that he might be connecting, Millford pushed on.

"I mean, wouldn't it make more sense for you to find someone in your same element? A handsome river, perhaps? Or maybe even the Rain King?"

A wave lapped against the boat in assent, and in the next moment, Slub Glub was on his feet, declaring authoritatively, "By the power invested in me as the minister of the Church of Slub Glub, I now pronounce you to no longer be man and…"

His sentence, however, was not to be finished, as at that very moment, a shrill, booming voice called out, "Halt that! Halt that immediately!" A shocked Millford turned around, and found his own mother staring back at him.

Chapter Sixty-Five

The Old Woman and The Sea

"Millford Phelonius Mutterwurst! Get aboard this instant!"

There she was, the stern, matronly figure of Mrs. Catipula Mutterwurst, her abundant form strangely attired in a striped shirt, pointy boots, and eyepatch. She was standing astride the bow of a rather large sailing vessel, complete with cannons pointed off the starboard side.

"Er, hello, mother," Millford replied, and he dutifully obeyed her. He stepped over Lumino's sinking carcass and hoisted himself up the ladder that Mrs. Mutterwurst tossed down to him. The monkey followed suit, making a last derogatory gesture towards the Speckled Hornswallow, whose difficult beak was still inappropriately stuck in the side of Lumino's flattened head.

Slub Glub eagerly hopped up to join them, extending a tentacle to their rescuer. "I am so pleased to meet you, Mrs. Mutterwurst! Millford's told me so much about you!" Actually, Millford hadn't told him anything about her, but Slub Glub was never quite clear on what someone might or might not have told him.

"Peculiar friends you've got these days, Millford," Mrs. Mutterwurst sneered. She then turned to face the sea, chiding, "Haven't you been looking after my boy? What kind of wife are you, anyway?"

Millford looked around the vessel. "So, Mother. You've become… a sailor?" There was an edge to his voice.

"Oh, yes indeed," she replied.

Chapter Sixty-Six

"Sail the Black Seas"
(Mrs. Catipula Mutterwurst's Sailing Song)

Head underwater
Swimming with belief
A thousand bright ideas
Smashed up on the reef

And you're a pearl
As pure as any world
As sweet as any novacaine

We're gonna wear black
We're gonna wave a white flag
And launch an attack
We're never coming back

Everybody
Everywhere
Sail the big black sea
Follow me

Chapter Sixty-Seven

This Flat Planet

Catipula Mutterwurst's boat was large and wooden, and contrary to her song, the flag it flew was as black as an eye socket.

"My god, boy, you look terrible!" She peered at him curiously for a moment, and then held out one of his gangling, twisted limbs. "Your elbows are flat as boards! And what's this?" She poked him in what used to be his stomach. "Caved in like an eggshell. Not to mention the eyebrows, or lack thereof. Good lord, son. If your hands got any smaller we could use 'em as nose-pickers!"

"Don't remind me," Millford groaned. "Maybe it's a dietary issue."

"In that case, it's nothing but limwhist sandwiches, from this day forth!"

At the mention of limwhist, Slub Glub perked up. "Limwhist? Did I hear someone say limwhist? I'll take two," he chirped, tentacles aflutter. Mrs. Mutterwurst eyed him skeptically.

"So what are you and your little friends doing out here? Were you reconciling with your spouse?"

"I could ask you the same question," Millford said bitterly, if incoherently.

"Now don't be cross, Millford. I can tell you're still miffed about that marriage thing. Well, I was merely looking out for you, setting you up with the sea. But I see that you two have drifted apart, even as we drift on top of her. Have you kids considered relationship counseling?"

"No, Mother. In fact, I'm seeing someone else."

"Oh." Mrs. Mutterwurst feigned nonchalance. "Anyone I know?"

"Not likely, Mother. I haven't talked to you for twenty-two years." He paused for impact. "You might tell me where you've been."

"You might say I've been right here. After the wedding, I knew that the sea," she made a sweeping gesture to the surrounding waters, "would take care of you… And I knew it would take care of me, too, in a way."

When she made that sweeping gesture, Millford noticed for the first time that a metal hook protruded from her right arm. "What happened to your hand?"

"Nothing. I wear it for effect." She pulled off the hook and extended her fingers from the inside of her blouse sleeve. "In my line of work, it can be useful."

"And what line of work is that?"

"Come down below, and I'll show you." She led him down a hatch in the deck. Slub Glub and the monkey stayed above, admiring the wooden figure that adorned the ship's prow: a figurehead of a mermaid, with three eyes no less, staring out in all directions across the waters.

Down below, the hold of the ship was cavernous and barren, except for a bunch of wooden crates. "I'm an importer-exporter," Mrs. Mutterwurst explained. She stood before a crate, prying one of its boards loose with her hook. "I sail from one end of this flat Earth to the other, bringing junk from here to there and then taking some junk back again." Reaching into the case, she pulled out a tea bag. "As of late, I mostly deal in tea."

105

Millford took a look. "That's the same brand I drink back home."

"Yes, I know."

"You know?"

"I talk to the sea, of course. We're together a lot. And the sea, naturally, is on very close terms with the rain. And the rain, my dear, eventually becomes the water you use to boil your tea."

"Oh."

"And I almost forgot. I have something here for you."

Chapter Sixty-Eight
The Garden of Early Delights

Mrs. Mutterwurst led her son over to the corner, where a musty footlocker sat in dilapidation. "You'll never guess what's in here," she said, inserting her hook in the padlock.

"Electric socks?"

"No."

"An eel magnifier?"

"No."

"Book warmers?"

"No! Just wait a minute, Millford!" With an irritated turn, the padlock broke. Mrs. Mutterwurst lifted the old footlocker's lid.

Millford gazed in wonder at what was inside. "My bug!" he exclaimed, pulling forth a stuffed beetle. Well worn, the toy's worn seams betrayed their interior stuffing. Millford brought the stuffed animal, which was nearly as old as he, to his face, and cuddled its snout, which was stiff from the seeping affections of the toddler he once had been.

"And my Pantaloon Brigade!" He reached in and extracted a set of strange little tin men. "I can't believe you saved all this!" The trunk was full of the beloved toys of Millford's childhood.

"Yep, they're all there, all your old things. Remember

this?" His mother handed him a creepy doll, with an elongated nose, whose hair was pulled atop her head in a waffle-like shape. "That used to be your favorite," Mrs. Mutterwurst reflected.

"Yes." Millford turned the doll around in his hand.

"You were quite the active youngster, Millford. Look at all that. You were always up to something new… Building your little collections." She paused in remembrance, seating her oblong bottom on one of the tea crates. "So tell me about yourself… What line of work are you in?"

"I'm a rock salesman."

"Rocks, eh? That's a good field." She looked at her son affectionately. "And what about your new lady friend?"

Millford looked at her, surprised, and his heart softened a little bit toward her, as hers had already done towards him… For whatever may have come between them, they were mother and son, and he had once come forth from inside her, though it was best not to think about that.

"Actually… We've had a fight."

Hearing a ruckus above deck (Slub Glub had slipped on a barnacle while chasing the monkey, who was scaling the rigging), Mrs. Mutterwurst left Millford alone with his thoughts.

Chapter Sixty-Nine

"Doll House Parade"
(A Song Sung From Inside the Toy Box)

Sat on the shelf where there's nobody else
That comes through the door anymore
Light in the hall but there's no one at all
And the shadows are stuntedly small

Sockets are stockings with seams unstitching
The eye is a button (just one)
Still after all is said and done a clay head is better than none

She used to dance, you can tell by her entrance
The wind-ups are playing her song along
The floor board and discord, the clown turns the key
In her back; it's the nerve that she lacks

Sockets are stockings with seams unstitching
The eye is a button (just one)
Still after all is said and done a clay head is better than none

The shape of a shade of the puppet brigade
Come to play in the doll house parade

Still after all is said and done a clay head is better than none

Chapter Seventy

The Lady in the Pool

Night had descended on the ship. The moon bobbed gently across the sky, like the bouncing ball in a vaudevillian sing-a-long.

Millford wasn't sleeping. He leaned over the side of the boat, staring at the reflection of the stars in the sea. As he stared, they seemed to coalesce into a watery approximation of Edweena's face.

"The sea," Millford thought, "is a big puddle of tears."

Chapter Seventy-One
Not Quite A Full Deck

Morning found Mrs. Mutterwurst, Slub Glub, and the monkey up early and feeling quite refreshed. Though they'd all slept on the hard floor of the boat, the lapping waves had been soothing. They now sat around the deck-side table, playing blackjack. The monkey was winning by a wide margin, and Mrs. Mutterwurst, who had a plug of tobacco lodged between teeth and gum, was getting a tad ticked off.

"Let's see your cards," she called, and Slub Glub displayed his hand proudly: a four of clubs, the king of spades, and a laundry receipt. "A Bathroom Flush," he jubilantly exclaimed. "I win."

Mrs. Mutterwurst spat in disgust.

Chapter Seventy-Two

Cruel Cargo Causes Complications

Millford joined the others at the card table. He had spent a sleepless night in the cargo hold, picking his life apart with tweezers. "You look terrible," his mother said. "Let's fix you a cup of tea." She turned to Slub Glub and asked him to fetch a case of tea bags from below.

Moments later, Slub Glub reappeared through the hatch, pushing a large crate ahead of him. Mrs. Mutterwurst grabbed a Bunsen burner and pot from her cabin and for the next two hours they all imbibed copiously.

It was when Millford got up to relieve himself that he found there was, once again, something terribly wrong. In attempting to walk to the lavatory (which, in this case, was just the side of the ship), he fell directly on his backside, and regained a standing position only with difficulty.

Upon rolling up his pant legs, he found to his dismay that his knees were reversed. They were now capped on the insides. Walking was difficult.

Millford, if not exactly pleased, was growing to accept his body's speedy and seemingly irreversible decline. He hobbled back to his family and friends, dragging his shins behind him. His return went unnoticed, however, as the monkey had just sighted a rowboat on the horizon.

Chapter Seventy-Three
The Caress of the Catatonic Castaway

"Whoop! Whoop!" the monkey called, balancing on the ship's prow, staring down at the flimsy vessel that was drifting listlessly alongside Mrs. Mutterwurst's ship.

"Why, it's Millford's pointy-nosed lady friend!" chirped Slub Glub. Indeed, Edweena Toadsweater lay inside the battered little boat, apparently alone, and apparently unconscious, if not worse.

As soon as Millford realized what was happening, he moved with alarming speed, backwards knees or not, and went down the rope ladder. He gathered Edweena in his arms.

Gazing at her elongated, immobile face, Millford felt himself overcome with emotion, and felt sure his heart would stop, if hers could not start.

Then she opened her eyes.

Chapter Seventy-Four

"Easy Virtue"
(Millford's Song for the Opening of Dead Hearts)

I was lodged in the poor house
Less to my name than a church mouse
Wandering through a maze of malaise

When you wave your six arms
I can't help but be charmed
Though I falter at the altar when I come to worship you

I hear a ding-dong-ding
The bells are ringing in my head
Like Quasimodo said

I hear a singing
A flock of angels taking wing
And they bring…

Easy virtue, coming through you, here at last

By fires on the hillside
And statues near the door

I've been deciphering the hieroglyphics you've been writing

All of your ideas that I used to find weird now I believe
Your sacrificial ritual, sacramental confessional
Smells like the truth to me

I thought that my stigmata was just more blood on my hands
But now I feel quite faultless and I just want you to be my god-
dess

I hear a ding-dong-ding
The bells are ringing in my head
Like Quasimodo said

I hear a singing
A flock of angels taking wing
And they bring

Easy virtue, coming through you, here at last
Leaking through the cracks like sun-stained glass will let light pass

Chapter Seventy-Five

The Invalid Accuser

"Oh, Millford, that was wonderful," Edweena gushed.

"I wrote it about a sandwich."

"You did not!"

They shared a peaceful moment, basking in the blush of renewed love.

It was, sorry to say, not to last, for in the next moment, a small, wooden voice croaked out, "Help!"

"What's that?" Millford wondered, and before Edweena could answer, the voice moaned again. It was coming from beneath the oars. Millford reached down, and found Grinnin' Gertie there.

"I'm dying," the puppet said, and although his hinged grin was still fixed in place, he did not look good. His painted cheeks were faded, and his limbs were as stiff as planks. His large eyes rolled with anguish, their painted pupils disturbingly opposed in direction.

Edweena had sufficiently recovered, so she climbed the ladder up the side of the ship, and Millford followed, holding the splayed and whining ventriloquist's dummy.

Millford laid Grinnin' Gertie down on the deck. "Hey! I've seen you on T.V!" Mrs. Mutterwurst exclaimed, but Grinnin' Gertie was in too much discomfort to acknowledge the compliment.

"O my," Slub Glub fretted. "This is not good. What happened? Was it a jellyfish? The aurora borealis?"

As the dummy struggled for breath, they all crowded around him, leaning in close. All, that is, but Edweena, who stood aside, looking nervous.

"She did this to me," groaned the puppet, pointing a shaky wooden finger towards Edweena.

Everyone turned to her with looks of bewilderment. She made no reply.

"It was the tea," the poor puppet croaked.

Silence descended on the little party as they all pondered this extraordinary statement. Millford wrung his hands with confusion, and in doing so, was reminded again of just how much they'd shrunk.

And then it was like the clouds had parted and a sickly black sun shone down upon him for the first time. He remembered the cups of tea he had drunk with Edweena, and the hideous disintegration that his body had succumbed to afterwards. The dots were connected in Millford's mind, and he turned with cold, accusing eyes to Edweena, whose face blanched with guilt.

Chapter Seventy-Six

"The Ballad of a Slow Poisoner"
(Edweena's Awful Admission)

Lean back your head
Drink in this medicine
I am a patient one
Piece by piece
The days drift into weeks
It takes time to disappear

You're too much for this world to see
Solution's easy
Simple chemistry
I won't let you be if you're not with me
And I've got time
Slip it in your wine

Sit back, relax
Sip from this green glass
Float on fields of arsenic
No one will know
They'll say you had to go
Silk feathers for the feast

I heard you had your portrait done
A good idea
You're getting weaker
Every day at ten to three
Please have your tea
I've made it sweet

You'll never wither, you'll never grow old
Always be fair as the day
Each knot in the rope, and each drop in the sea
Bringing you closer to me
Winds whisper strychnine and pigeons in pies
Pennies placed over your eyes
Pockets of posy when thin as a dime
Trepanning into your mind
Hand made of paper and faces of lace
Falling behind in the race
A touch of elixir our thoughts are erased
Vanishing without a trace

Lean back your head, drink in this medicine
I am a patient one

Chapter Seventy-Seven

A Disturbing Disclosure

Her melodious admission ended, Edweena burst solidly into tears. Slub Glub, who had the peculiar habit of bursting into tears himself whenever anyone near him was crying, did the same.

"Oh, Millford, I'm so sorry…" Edweena sobbed.

"Edweena, why did you do it?" Millford asked.

"Because if I can't have you, then no one can!"

"That's original," interjected Mrs. Mutterwurst.

Millford shot his mother an angry glance, then turned sympathetically to Edweena. "Edweena, I'm divorcing the sea."

"Oh, Millford!" she exclaimed, and ran to his arms. "That must be why she let us drift back together…"

They all sat down around the card table, and Edweena made a full confession. "I knew it was wrong, but I was just so mad with love for you. I plucked those awful berries from your backyard, and mixed them up with your tea in my kettle."

"Witch!" groaned the dummy, who was still recuperating on the floor of the ship.

"How come you weren't poisoned, too?" Millford asked.

"When you weren't looking, I would spit the tea into my armpit. See?" She lifted up her arm, and all assembled groaned at the grunginess of its pit. "Oh Millford, can you ever see fit to forgive me?"

"I do."

"it's all so terribly wonderful" cried Slub Glub, bawling even harder.

Chapter Seventy-Eight

The Captain Comes Clean As Well

"I'm sorry to interrupt this tender moment," said Mrs. Mutterwurst, "But Edweena, does this tea bag look familiar?" She was pointing to an open crate of the tea bags that were her vessel's cargo.

"Why, that's the tea I poisoned," Edweena affirmed.

"Then you should not blame yourself alone," Mrs. Mutterwurst said. Millford looked quizically at his mother. "I, too, have been tampering with tea," she explained. "As the chief stateside importer of this particular brand, I've taken it upon myself to enhance every shipment with a liberal sprinkling of great spiders and diamond powder. Deadly poisons, as you know."

"Why, Mother, that's terrible!"

"Yes," she said, hanging her head sadly. "I am a bitter old fool. My seafaring life has made me twisted and cruel."

She looked so pathetic, with a tear dripping down from behind her eye patch, that Slub Glub came over and hugged her, snot running down from his blue nose and onto her striped shirt.

"But you drank that tea yourself," Millford noted. "Why weren't you poisoned?"

"I was. Why do you think I wear this eye patch! And what's more…" She parted her stringy hair and revealed a marked concavity at the back of her skull, as if someone had impressed a battering ram into her head.

124

Slub Glub suddenly fell silent, his tiny mind turning over something with alarm. "Great spiders and diamond powder?" he asked in a small voice.

Chapter Seventy-Nine

Hapless Blue Thing

"B-but but but..." he sobbed, and he reached his tentacle into his little wicker basket, pulling out a quantity of shiny dust.

"That's the stuff. That's diamond powder, just like I used," Mrs. Mutterwurst noted. Slub Glub reached in again, this time extracting a particularly obnoxious eight-legged insect. "And that's a great spider, alright," Millford's mom confirmed.

"I thought they were just spices!" Slub Glub moaned, flapping his tentacles with such angst that Edweena was compelled to put her arm around what passed for his shoulders. "I always put them in my tea! I didn't think they were dangerous... Just zesty!"

"Oh, they're fatal, alright," Mrs. Mutterwurst opined.

"I'm a murderer!" Slub Glub blubbered.

"But you were drinking that tea with me while we were in the balloon! How come you're not disintegrating?" Millford asked. Slub Glub looked at him with woeful, glassy eyes, and explained, "I can't be poisoned! I have no insides."

Millford turned to the monkey. "I hope you weren't trying to kill me too."

"Whoop whoop," the monkey said.

Chapter Eighty

All's Well Enough That Ends Well Enough

With the air now cleared, a certain calm prevailed. Everyone agreed that Millford would certainly recover, provided that no more deadly toxins were to enter his system. And Millford, for his part, proved to be exceedingly understanding about the whole business. Therefore, off they sailed, drifting slowly westward, with their troubled pasts sinking surely behind them.

Grinnin' Gertie, the ventriloquist's dummy, recovered from his internal rotting and fell in love with the three-eyed mermaid that adorned the prow of Mrs. Mutterwurst's ship. He affixed himself to the wooden figurehead's side, and was never to leave.

Mrs. Catipula Mutterwurst, having been reunited with Millford, found that the hole in her head had become filled. She no longer tainted the tea she transported, and in fact discounted the price. She continued to sail across the seas of this flat Earth, and had the able assistance of the monkey, whose faded green appearance blended nicely with the blues of the sea over which they floated.

Millford and Edweena, now free to be wed, did so the following night, in a sentimental ceremony that Slub Glub presided over. As for Slub Glub himself, he was taken in by the newlywedded couple as a gardener, and he moved into a hole that he dug in the backyard of the Mutterwurst residence.

Most significantly, the three of them switched to drinking coffee, and faced their future healthy and happy, if slightly agitated and overly-awake.

The End!

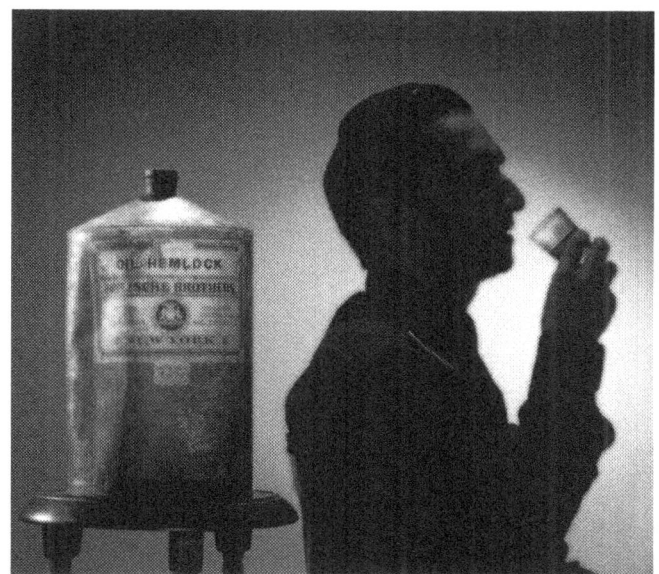

ABOUT THE AUTHOR

Andrew Goldfarb currently suffers from acute myopia and an inflammation of the olfactory organs. He is reputed to be buried in San Francisco, with occasional resurrections in New Orleans. He performs as a one man surrealistic rock and roll band under the moniker The Slow Poisoner, singing songs of will-o-the-wisps and woebegone wretches (www.theslowpoisoner.com). Andrew is also the author of the long-running comix art melodrama "Ogner Stump's One Thousand Sorrows," of which the first eighty-six have been completed (www.ognerstump.com). Mr. Goldfarb intends to go over Niagra Falls in a barrel at the age of one hundred.

Bizarro books

CATALOGUE – SPRING 2007

Bizarro Books publishes under the following imprints:

www.rawdogscreamingpress.com

www.eraserheadpress.com

www.afterbirthbooks.com

www.swallowdownpress.com

For all your Bizarro needs visit:

WWW.BIZARROCENTRAL.COM

BB-0X1   "The Bizarro Starter Kit"
An introduction to the Bizarro genre

There's a new genre rising out of the underground. Its name: BIZARRO. For years, readers have been asking for a category of fiction dedicated to the weird, crazy, cult side of storytelling that has become a staple in the film industry (with directors such as David Lynch, Takashi Miike, Tim Burton, and Lloyd Kaufman) but has been largely ignored in the literary world, until now.

THE BIZARRO STARTER KIT features short novels and story collections by ten of the leading authors in the genre: D. Harlan Wilson, Carlton Mellick III, Jeremy Robert Johnson, Kevin L Donihe, Gina Ranalli, Andre Duza, Vincent W. Sakowski, Steve Beard, John Edward Lawson, and Bruce Taylor. Get the perfect sampling of Bizarro for only five dollars plus shipping.

236 pages $5

  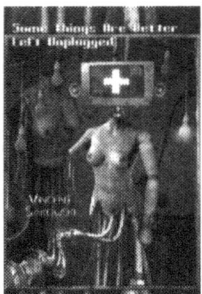 

BB-001"**The Kafka Effekt**" D. Harlan Wilson - A collection of forty-four irreal short stories loosely written in the vein of Franz Kafka, with more than a pinch of William S. Burroughs sprinkled on top. **211 pages** **$14**

BB-002 "**Satan Burger**" Carlton Mellick III - The cult novel that put Carlton Mellick III on the map ... Six punks get jobs at a fast food restaurant owned by the devil in a city violently overpopulated by surreal alien cultures. **236 pages** **$14**

BB-003 "**Some Things Are Better Left Unplugged**" Vincent Sakwoski - Join The Man and his Nemesis, the obese tabby, for a nightmare roller coaster ride into this postmodern fantasy. **152 pages** **$10**

BB-004 "**Shall We Gather At the Garden?**" Kevin L Donihe - Donihe's Debut novel. Midgets take over the world, The Church of Lionel Richie vs. The Church of the Byrds, plant porn and more! **244 pages** **$14**

   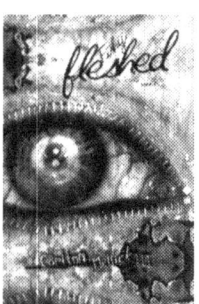

BB-005 "**Razor Wire Pubic Hair**" Carlton Mellick III - A genderless humandildo is purchased by a razor dominatrix and brought into her nightmarish world of bizarre sex and mutilation. **176 pages** **$11**

BB-006 "**Stranger on the Loose**" D. Harlan Wilson - The fiction of Wilson's 2nd collection is planted in the soil of normalcy, but what grows out of that soil is a dark, witty, otherworldly jungle... **228 pages** **$14**

BB-007 "**The Baby Jesus Butt Plug**" Carlton Mellick III - Using clones of the Baby Jesus for anal sex will be the hip sex fetish of the future. **92 pages** **$10**

BB-008 "**Fishyfleshed**" Carlton Mellick III - The world of the past is an illogical flatland lacking in dimension and color, a sick-scape of crispy squid people wandering the desert for no apparent reason. **260 pages** **$14**

BB-009 **"Dead Bitch Army"** Andre Duza - Step into a world filled with racist teenagers, cannibals, 100 warped Uncle Sams, automobiles with razor-sharp teeth, living graffiti, and a pissed-off zombie bitch out for revenge. **344 pages $16**

BB-010 **"The Menstruating Mall"** Carlton Mellick III *"The Breakfast Club* meets *Chopping Mall* as directed by David Lynch."* - Brian Keene **212 pages $12**

BB-011 **"Angel Dust Apocalypse"** Jeremy Robert Johnson - Meth-heads, man-made monsters, and murderous Neo-Nazis. "Seriously amazing short stories..." - Chuck Palahniuk, author of *Fight Club* **184 pages $11**

BB-012 **"Ocean of Lard"** Kevin L Donihe / Carlton Mellick III - A parody of those old Choose Your Own Adventure kid's books about some very odd pirates sailing on a sea made of animal fat. **176 pages $12**

   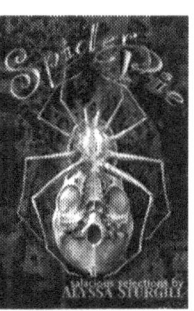

BB-013 **"Last Burn in Hell"** John Edward Lawson - From his lurid angst-affair with a lesbian music diva to his ascendance as unlikely pop icon the one constant for Kenrick Brimley, official state prison gigolo, is he's got no clue what he's doing. **172 pages $14**

BB-014 **"Tangerinephant"** Kevin Dole 2 - TV-obsessed aliens have abducted Michael Tangerinephant in this bizarre combination of science fiction, satire, and surrealism. **164 pages $11**

BB-015 **"Foop!"** Chris Genoa - Strange happenings are going on at Dactyl, Inc, the world's first and only time travel tourism company.
"A surreal pie in the face!" - Christopher Moore **300 pages $14**

BB-016 **"Spider Pie"** Alyssa Sturgill - A one-way trip down a rabbit hole inhabited by sexual deviants and friendly monsters, fairytale beginnings and hideous endings. **104 pages $11**

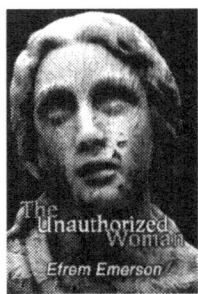   

BB-017 **"The Unauthorized Woman"** Efrem Emerson - Enter the world of the inner freak, a landscape populated by the pre-dead and morticioners, by cockroaches and 300-lb robots. **104 pages $11**

BB-018 **"Fugue XXIX"** Forrest Aguirre - Tales from the fringe of speculative literary fiction where innovative minds dream up the future's uncharted territories while mining forgotten treasures of the past. **220 pages $16**

BB-019 **"Pocket Full of Loose Razorblades"** John Edward Lawson - A collection of dark bizarro stories. From a giant rectum to a foot-fungus factory to a girl with a biforked tongue. **190 pages $13**

BB-020 **"Punk Land"** Carlton Mellick III - In the punk version of Heaven, the anarchist utopia is threatened by corporate fascism and only Goblin, Mortician's sperm, and a blue-mohawked female assassin named Shark Girl can stop them. **284 pages $15**

BB-021 **"Pseudo-City"** D. Harlan Wilson - Pseudo-City exposes what waits in the bathroom stall, under the manhole cover and in the corporate boardroom, all in a way that can only be described as mind-bogglingly irreal. **220 pages $16**

BB-022 **"Kafka's Uncle and Other Strange Tales"** Bruce Taylor - Anslenot and his giant tarantula (tormentor? fri-end?) wander a desecrated world in this novel and collection of stories from Mr. Magic Realism Himself. **348 pages $17**

BB-023 **"Sex and Death In Television Town"** Carlton Mellick III - In the old west, a gang of hermaphrodite gunslingers take refuge from a demon plague in Telos: a town where its citizens have televisions instead of heads. **184 pages $12**

BB-024 **"It Came From Below The Belt"** Bradley Sands - What can Grover Goldstein do when his severed, sentient penis forces him to return to high school and help it win the presidential election? **204 pages $13**

BB-025 "Sick: An Anthology of Illness" John Lawson, editor - These Sick stories are horrendous and hilarious dissections of creative minds on the scalpel's edge. **296 pages $16**

BB-026 "Tempting Disaster" John Lawson, editor - A shocking and alluring anthology from the fringe that examines our culture's obsession with taboos. **260 pages $16**

BB-027 "Siren Promised" Jeremy Robert Johnson - Nominated for the Bram Stoker Award. A potent mix of bad drugs, bad dreams, brutal bad guys, and surreal/incredible art by Alan M. Clark. **190 pages $13**

BB-028 "Chemical Gardens" Gina Ranalli - Ro and punk band *Green is the Enemy* find Kreepkins, a surfer-dude warlock, a vengeful demon, and a Metal Priestess in their way as they try to escape an underground nightmare. **188 pages $13**

  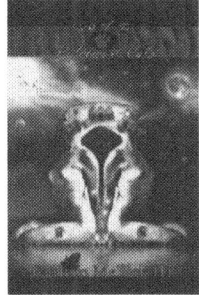 

BB-029 "Jesus Freaks" Andre Duza For God so loved the world that he gave his only two begotten sons… and a few million zombies. **400 pages $16**

BB-030 "Grape City" Kevin L. Donihe - More Donihe-style comedic bizarro about a demon named Charles who is forced to work a minimum wage job on Earth after Hell goes out of business. **108 pages $10**

BB-031"Sea of the Patchwork Cats" Carlton Mellick III - A quiet dreamlike tale set in the ashes of the human race. For Mellick enthusiasts who also adore *The Twilight Zone*. **112 pages $10**

BB-032 "Extinction Journals" Jeremy Robert Johnson - An uncanny voyage across a newly nuclear America where one man must confront the problems associated with loneliness, insane dieties, radiation, love, and an ever-evolving cockroach suit with a mind of its own. **104 pages $10**

BB-033 "Meat Puppet Cabaret" Steve Beard At last! The secret connection between Jack the Ripper and Princess Diana's death revealed! **240 pages $16 / $30**

BB-034 "The Greatest Fucking Moment in Sports" Kevin L. Donihe - In the tradition of the surreal anti-sitcom *Get A Life* comes a tale of triumph and agape love from the master of comedic bizarro. **108 pages $10**

BB-035 "The Troublesome Amputee" John Edward Lawson - Disturbing verse from a man who truly believes nothing is sacred and intends to prove it. **104 pages $9**

BB-036 "Deity" Vic Mudd God (who doesn't like to be called "God") comes down to a typical, suburban, Ohio family for a little vacation—but it doesn't turn out to be as relaxing as He had hoped it would be... **168 pages $12**

  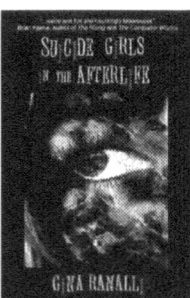 

BB-037 "The Haunted Vagina" Carlton Mellick III - It's difficult to love a woman whose vagina is a gateway to the world of the dead. **132 pages $10**

BB-038 "Tales from the Vinegar Wasteland" Ray Fracalossy - Witness: a man is slowly losing his face, a neighbor who periodically screams out for no apparent reason, and a house with a room that doesn't actually exist. **240 pages $14**

BB-039 "Suicide Girls in the Afterlife" Gina Ranalli - After Pogue commits suicide, she unexpectedly finds herself an unwilling "guest" at a hotel in the Afterlife, where she meets a group of bizarre characters, including a goth Satan, a hippie Jesus, and an alien-human hybrid. **100 pages $9**

BB-040 "And Your Point Is?" Steve Aylett - In this follow-up to LINT multiple authors provide critical commentary and essays about Jeff Lint's mind-bending literature. **104 pages $11**

 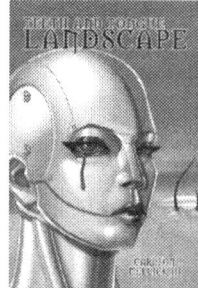  

BB-041 "Not Quite One of the Boys" Vincent Sakowski -While drug-dealer Maxi drinks with Dante in purgatory, God and Satan play a little tri-level chess and do a little bargaining over his business partner, Vinnie, who is still left on earth. **220 pages $14**

BB-042 "Teeth and Tongue Landscape" Carlton Mellick III - On a planet made out of meat, a socially-obsessive monophobic man tries to find his place amongst the strange creatures and communities that he comes across. **110 pages $10**

BB-043 "War Slut" Carlton Mellick III - Part "1984," part "Waiting for Godot," and part action horror video game adaptation of John Carpenter's "The Thing." **116 pages $10**

BB-044 "All Encompassing Trip" Nicole Del Sesto -In a world where coffee is no longer available, the only television shows are reality TV re-runs, and the animals are talking back, Nikki, Amber and a singing Coyote in a do-rag are out to restore the light **308 pages $15**

BB-045 "Dr. Identity" D. Harlan Wilson - Follow the Dystopian Duo on a killing spree of epic proportions through the irreal postcapitalist city of Bliptown where time ticks sideways, artificial Bug-Eyed Monsters punish citizens for consumer-capitalist lethargy, and ultraviolence is as essential as a daily multivitamin. **208 pages $15**

BB-046 "The Million-Year Centipede" Vincent Sakowski -Wakelin, frontman for 'The Hinge,' wrote a poem so prophetic that to ignore it dooms a person to drown in blood. **130 pages $12**

BB-047 "Sausagey Santa" Carlton Mellick III - A bizarro Christmas tale featuring Santa as a piratey mutant with a body made of sausages. **124 pages $10**

BB-048 "Misadventures in a Thumbnail Universe" Vincent Sakowski - Dive deep into the surreal and satirical realms of neo-classical Blender Fiction, filled with television shoes and flesh-filled skies. **120 pages $10**

BB-049 **"Vacation"** **Jeremy C. Shipp** - Blueblood Bernard Johnson leaves his boring life behind to go on The Vacation, a year-long corporate sponsored odyssey. But instead of seeing the world, Bernard is captured by terrorists, becomes a key figure in secret drug wars, and, worse, doesn't once miss his secure American Dream. **160 pages** **$14**

BB-050 **"Discouraging at Best"** **John Edward Lawson** - A collection where the absurdity of the mundane expands exponentially creating a tidal wave that sweeps reason away. For those who enjoy satire, bizarro, or a good old-fashioned slap to the senses. **208 pages** **$15**

BB-051 **"13 Thorns"** **Gina Ranalli** - Thirteen tales of twisted, bizarro horror. **240 pages** **$13**

BB-052 **"Better Ways of Being Dead"** **Christian TeBordo** - In this class, the students have to keep one palm down on the table at all times, and listen to lectures about a panda who speaks Chinese. Surely there must be a better way to get health insurance to cover his chronic congenital dermatitis... **216 pages** **$14**

COMING SOON

"House of Houses" by Kevin Donihe

"The Faggiest Vampire" by Carlton Mellick III

"Super Cell Anemia" by Duncan Barlow

"Wall of Kiss" by Gina Ranalli

"Cocoon Of Terror" by Jason Earls

"HELP! A Bear is Eating Me!" by Mykle Hansen

ORDER FORM

TITLES	QTY	PRICE	TOTAL

Please make checks and moneyorders payable to ROSE O'KEEFE / BIZARRO BOOKS in U.S. funds only. Please don't send bad checks! Allow 2-6 weeks for delivery. International orders may take longer. If you'd like to pay online via PAYPAL.COM, send payments to publisher@eraserheadpress.com.

SHIPPING: US ORDERS - $2 for the first book, $1 for each additional book. For priority shipping, add an additional $4. INT'L ORDERS - $5 for the first book, $3 for each additional book. Add an additional $5 per book for global priority shipping.

Send payment to:

BIZARRO BOOKS
 C/O Rose O'Keefe
 205 NE Bryant
 Portland, OR 97211

Address	
City	State Zip
Email	Phone